THE BIG BOOK OF BUSH

CARTOONS!

Edited by
Daryl Cagle and
Brian Fairrington

ENRON

Dedication

This book is dedicated to the tremendously talented artists at Politicalcartoons.com and our hard working staff at Cagle Cartoons, Cari Dawson Bartley, Brian Davis and Stacey Fairrington, who work tirelessly to promote the art of political cartoons.

The BIG Book of BUSH Cartoons

Daryl Cagle, Cartoonist-Editor, Cover

Brian Fairrington, Cartoonist-Editor, Inside-Front Cover

Susan Cagle, Writer/Editor

Stacey Fairrington, Layout/Editor

Cari Dawson Bartley, Marketing for Cagle Cartoons

Laura Norman, Executive Editor for Que Publishing

International Standard Book Number: 0-7897-3470-2
Library of Congress Catalog Card Number: 2005930260
Printed in the United States of America
First Printing: October 2005

THE BIG BOOK OF BUSH CARTOONS

Table of Contents

About This Book

We've assembled many of the best political cartoonists in the world to tell the story of the Bush administration in cartoons. We run the colossal website at politicalcartoons.com that features all the newest and best political cartoons by all the best cartoonists. For the past six years, our website has been all about President Bush. In fact, every political cartoonist feels like he is drawing a little comic strip with President Bush as the main character.

Our *BIG Book of BUSH Cartoons* is organized like our website, with a chapter on each major event during the Bush presidency. Each chapter could have been a book on its own. The Bush administration has seen tumultuous times—the 9/11 attacks, the wars in Afghanistan and Iraq, worldwide terrorism from London to Madrid to Bali—with new controversies at every turn. The president is a great cartoon character, and he surrounds himself with other characters who create a cast that is richer than any cartoonist could dream up on his own.

Our book comes out when the president still has much of his second term in front of him, and he is still the central character on the national stage. This is a storybook about George W. Bush the cartoon character. This is also a history book, with cartoons reflecting our thoughts, feelings, and reactions to the events taking place over six turbulent years.

This book has not been put together with any partisan bias, but readers will detect a liberal perspective in the cartoons. Most political cartoonists are liberal, but even the few conservative cartoonists are critical of President Bush. In politics it is easy to poke fun at the people in power. Political cartooning is a negative art form. Cartoonists tear things down. There is nothing funny about a cartoon that defends the people in power. Our book may seem like a chorus of criticism against the president, but our selection is a representative sampling of what the cartoons were really like at this time.

Our book is biased because all of our contributors are biased. President Bush is both our protagonist and our target. We love him and hate him—this is the nature of the Bush presidency. We were torn apart by our disagreements, drawn together by sorrow and national pride; we were richer and poorer, happier and angrier. President Bush brought out the extremes in America, and those extremes are illustrated beautifully by the cartoons.

Daryl Cagle

About the Editor-Cartoonists

Daryl Cagle

Daryl is the daily editorial cartoonist for MSNBC.com. With more than three million regular, unique users each month, Daryl's editorial cartoon site with Microsoft (www.cagle.com) is the most popular cartoon website, of any kind, on the Internet. It is also the most widely used education site in social studies classrooms around the world.

For the past 30 years, Daryl has been one of America's most prolific cartoonists. Raised in California, Daryl went to college at UC Santa Barbara, then moved to New York City where he worked for 10 years with *Jim Henson's Muppets,* illustrating scores of books, magazines, calendars and all manner of products.

In 2001, Daryl started a new syndicate, *Cagle Cartoons, Inc.* (www.caglecartoons.com and www.politicalcartoons.com), which distributes the cartoons of 40 editorial cartoonists and columnists to more than 800 newspapers in the U.S., Canada, and Latin America. Daryl is a past president of the *National Cartoonists Society.* He has been married for 22 years and has two lovely children, Susan and Michael.

Brian Fairrington

Brian is one of the most accomplished young cartoonists in the country. While at Arizona State University, Brian won the John Locher Memorial Award from the Association of American Editorial Cartoonists. He also won the Charles M. Schulz Award from the Scripps Howard Foundation as the best college cartoonist. Since turning pro, Brian has gathered a bunch of new, glittering, cartooning trophies.

Brian works as a contributing political cartoonist for the *Arizona Republic* and his cartoons are nationally syndicated to more than 800 newspapers by *Cagle Cartoons* (www.caglecartoons.com). FOX News named a cartoon of his as "number one" in their best cartoons of the year countdown.

Brian is married to Stacey Heywood and they have three children. Besides drawing, his hobbies include performing turn-of-the-century Russian dental procedures on abandoned mountain gorillas and mounting stuffed brown squirrels on pieces of dry driftwood.

Cagle portrait by Cagle; Fairrington Portrait by Fairrington

We Want to Hear from You!

As the reader of this book, you are our most important critic and commentator. We value your opinion and want to know what we're doing right, what we could do better, what areas you'd like to see us publish in, and any other words of wisdom you're willing to pass our way.

As an associate publisher for Que Publishing, I welcome your comments. You can email or write me directly to let me know what you did or didn't like about this book—as well as what we can do to make our books better.

When you write, please be sure to include this book's title and author as well as your name, email address, and phone number. I will carefully review your comments and share them with the author and editors who worked on the book.

Email: feedback@quepublishing.com

Mail: Greg Wiegand
      Associate Publisher
      Que Publishing
      800 East 96th Street
      Indianapolis, IN 46240 USA

For more information about this book or another Que Publishing title, visit our Web site at www.quepublishing.com. Type the ISBN (excluding hyphens) or the title of a book in the Search field to find the page you're looking for.

How to Draw George W. Bush

Political cartoonists are not much different from comic strip cartoonists; both draw an ongoing daily soap opera featuring a regular cast of characters. While comic strip cartoonists invent their own characters, the political cartoonist's characters are given to him by events in the world; we are all drawing our own little daily sagas starring the same main character, President Bush.

Around the world, cartoonists almost always draw President Bush as a cowboy. Outside America, a Texas cowboy is seen as uneducated, ill-mannered, a "trigger-happy marshal" or outlaw who is prone to violence. Cowboy depictions of the president by worldwide cartoonists are meant to be insults, but

HOW I DRAW GEORGE W. BUSH SO THAT I GET MY CARTOONS...

REPRINTED in EUROPE

MAKE HIM A COWBOY (THEY LOVE COWBOYS IN EUROPE.)

BIG HEAD.

CONFUSED EXPRESSION

Pea size Brain (PEOPLE ARE WISER IN EUROPE.)

POLICEMAN TO THE WORLD.

Really →BiG← GUNS

Big ears...to emphasize how Americans descended from apes.

NOTHING TO SHOOT AT.

ITCHY Trigger FINGERS YOU NEVER KNOW WHEN HE'S GONNA SHOOT!!

DARYL CAGLE SLATE.COM

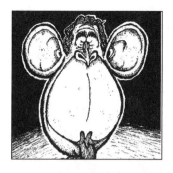

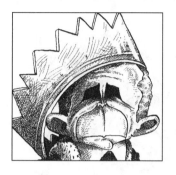

Americans see cowboys differently. In the USA, cowboys are noble, independent souls, living a romantic lifestyle by taming the wilderness and taking matters into their own hands whenever they see a wrong that needs to be righted. We are a nation of wanna-be cowboys.

The image of President Bush evolves with each cartoonist's personal perspective. Bush started out as most political cartoon characters start out, as a caricature of a real person, meant to be recognizable from a photograph. As time goes by, the cartoonists stop looking at photographs and start doing drawings of drawings, then drawings of drawings of drawings, so that the George W. Bush drawings morph into strangely deformed characters that look nothing like the real man, but are instantly recognizable because we've come to know the drawings as a symbol of the man. It is surprising that each cartoonist's drawings of the president look entirely different, but each is easily recognizable as representing the same character.

For some cartoonists, the president's ears have grown huge; a strange phenomenon, since the president doesn't have unusually large ears and isn't well known for listening. Some cartoonists have reduced President Bush in height. A combination of these has the president sometimes looking like a little bunny rabbit.

The president who shrank most in cartoons was Jimmy Carter. At the end of Carter's term he was a Munchkin, standing below knee height on almost every cartoonist's drawing table. President Bush has shrunk for only some of the more liberal cartoonists. President Reagan grew taller during his cartoon term in office. President Clinton grew fatter, even as he lost weight in real life. Bill Clinton's personality was fat, and the cartoonists drew the personality rather than the man. President Clinton is now skinny, but he will always be fat in cartoons.

Another cartoon characteristic that has grown from years of drawing President Bush are his eyes, two little dots, close together, topped by raised, quizzical eyebrows. The close, dotted eyes are an interesting universal phenomenon, shared by almost every cartoonist, that doesn't relate to the president's actual features. Over time, most cartoonists will draw a character with eyes that grow larger, but President Bush's eyes shrink, while his ears grow. There may be a political message in that, but I can't figure it out.

I once played "Political Cartoonist Name That Tune." The game went like this:

"I can draw President Bush in SIX LINES."

"Well, I can draw President Bush in FOUR LINES!"

"I can draw President Bush in THREE LINES!"

"OK. Draw that president!"

…and I did, two little dots topped by a raised, quizzical eyebrow line. It looked just like him.

Daryl Cagle

Campaign 2000

The 2000 presidential election was marked by lackluster debates between the two hopefuls: Bill Clinton's wooden Vice President Al Gore, and former president George Bush's cowboy son from Yale, who was known as "W." For the first time in U.S. history, the real debate began after the election when the outcome was unclear—the numbers on both sides were too close to call without counting every single ballot. Florida hung in the balance; and as officials from all over the state held disputed ballots up to high-intensity lights and adjusted their glasses, "hanging chad" became a familiar phrase in households across America.

The first counts showed Bush winning by a few hundred votes, but Gore sued for a recount. The case went all the way to the Supreme Court, which voted along party lines and handed Bush the presidency—despite accounts from Southern Florida that African-American voters had found themselves "mistakenly" disenfranchised by a state government headed by W.'s brother Jeb. And while Bush claimed to be "a uniter, not a divider," and promised a smooth transition, political cartoonists, along with half of America, had already caught a whiff of the changing winds.

DARYL CAGLE
Honolulu Advertiser

JEFF PARKER, Florida Today

J.D. CROWE
Mobile Register

'AND THE NEXT LEADER OF THE FREE WORLD IS...'

PETER LEWIS
Australia

JOHN TREVER
Albuquerque Journal

J.D. CROWE
Mobile Register

MIKE LANE, Baltimore Sun

MIKE LANE, Baltimore Sun

MONTE WOLVERTON, Cagle Cartoons

JEFF PARKER, Florida Today

JOHN TREVER, Albuquerque Journal

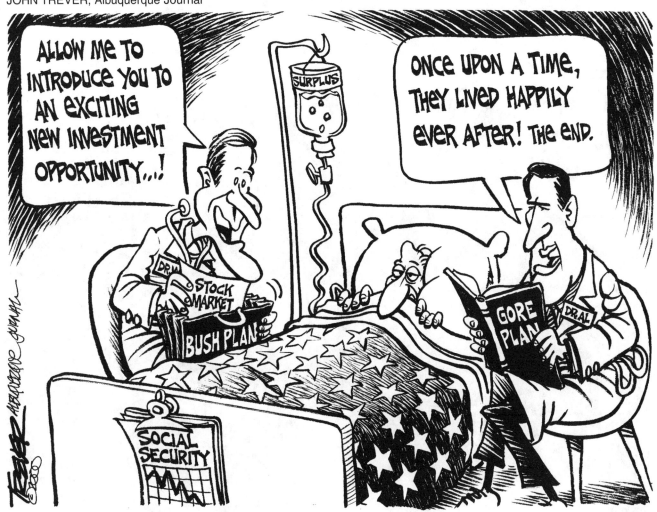

MIKE KEEFE
Denver Post

MONTE WOLVERTON
Cagle Cartoons

MIKE LANE, Baltimore Sun

JOHN TREVER
Albuquerque Journal

DON'T BE UN-AMERICAN, VOTE REPUBLICAN.

PLAYING POLITICS WITH NATIONAL SECURITY? NONSENSE.

WAR IS PEACE

SEAL OF THE PRESIDENT OF THE UNITED STATES

caglecartoons.com

JEFF PARKER, Florida Today

Dr. Bush's Amazing Texan Injection

Guaranteed to Cure All Societal Ills: Homocide, Mayhem, Larceny, Welfare Abuse, Wrong-Headedness, Minorities, Gun Control, MTV, Al Gore, etc., etc.

©2000 MONTE WOLVERTON

APPARENTLY, U.S. VOTERS' CHOICE IN 2000: OAK OR COKE

WOOHOO!

PARTY!

©1999 MONTE WOLVERTON

MONTE WOLVERTON
Cagle Cartoons

LOCK BOX

DARYL CAGLE
Midweek, Hawaii
www.cagle.com/hawaii

J.D. CROWE, Mobile Register

GREAT DEBATE EXPECTATIONS

EMAD HAJJAJ, Al-Ghad
Amman, Jordan

THE THOUSAND-POINTS-OF-LIGHT CAMPAIGN

THE DIM BULB CAMPAIGN

MIKE LANE, Cagle Cartoons

MIKE KEEFE, Denver Post

LARRY WRIGHT, Detroit News

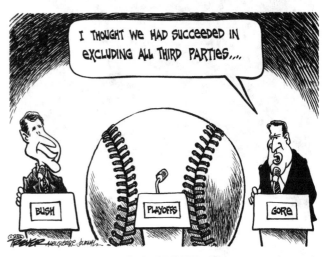

JOHN TREVER, Albuquerque Journal

J.D. CROWE, Mobile Register

JOHN TREVER
Albuquerque Journal

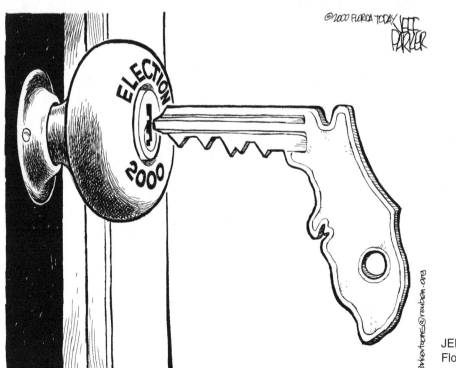

JEFF PARKER
Florida Today

JEFF PARKER
Florida Today

JOHN TREVER, Albuquerque Journal

MIKE KEEFE, Denver Post

JOHN TREVER
Albuquerque Journal

THE FAT LADY ...

CAMERON CARDOW
Ottawa Citizen

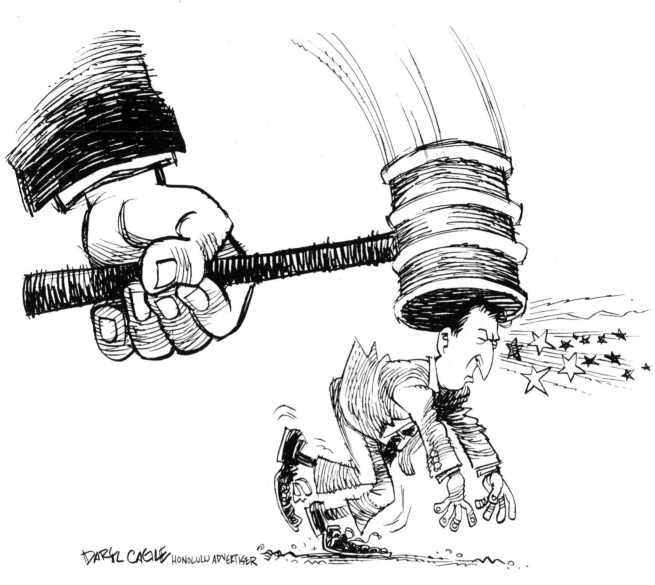

The election is over,
It's finished, it's through,
So clean up your mess now,
Thing One and Thing Two.

DARYL CAGLE
Honolulu Advertiser

R.J. MATSON, The New York Observer

MIKE LANE
Baltimore Sun

MIKE KEEFE
Denver Post

Bush and the Environment

President Bush was good to his environmentalist friends in the oil and timber industries ... and global warming? What's that?

DARYL CAGLE
Honolulu Advertiser

DARYL CAGLE www.cagle.com
HONOLULU ADVERTISER daryl@cagle.com

24

COURT UPHOLDS POLLUTION STANDARDS

SHOWERS →

GRUMBLE GRUMBLE.

W

MIKE LANE, Baltimore Sun

MONTE WOLVERTON
Cagle Cartoons

NATIONAL FORESTS

FOREST MANAGEMENT

REGS

IMPACT STATEMENTS

RED TAPE

APPEALS

LAWSUITS

THERE'S BEEN A DANGEROUS BUILDUP OF DEADWOOD... WE'RE PRESCRIBING A CONTROLLED BURN!

W

THINNING POLICY

JOHN TREVER
Albuquerque Journal

25

DARYL CAGLE
Honolulu Advertiser

MILT PRIGGEE

Some day, son, all this will be your problem

NIK SCOTT, Australia

MONTE WOLVERTON, Cagle Cartoons

BUSH INTRODUCES BOLD REFORESTATION PLAN:

PAT BAGLEY, Salt Lake Tribune

SANDY HUFFAKER, Cagle Cartoons

MONTE WOLVERTON, Cagle Cartoons

DARYL CAGLE, Slate

MIKE KEEFE, Denver Post

BUSH AND THE ENVIRONMENT

MONTE WOLVERTON
Cagle Cartoons

MIKE LANE
Baltimore Sun

PAT BAGLEY, Salt Lake Tribune

31

WWJD: "WHERE WOULD JESUS DRILL?"

CAMERON CARDOW
Ottawa Citizen

LARRY WRIGHT
Detroit News

32

MONTE WOLVERTON, Cagle Cartoons

MONTE WOLVERTON, Cagle Cartoons

DARYL CAGLE
Slate.com

33

Bush and Big Business

President George W. Bush has been a long-time friend to big business. Cartoonists see big business as a big bad guy looking for tax breaks and government handouts, and the president's close ties to his corporate buddies gave critics lots of fodder in the years when crooked CEOs brought down Worldcom, Tyco, and Arthur Anderson. Vice President Cheney had been the president of the giant contracting company Halliburton, which made a fortune from "no-bid government contracts" in Iraq. Big business had a big hand in the Bush administration.

PATRICK CHAPPATTE, International Herald Tribune

JEFF PARKER, Florida Today

SANDY HUFFAKER, Cagle Cartoons

JOHN TREVER, Albuquerque Journal

MIKE LANE, Baltimore Sun

Bad Santa

DARYL CAGLE, Slate

PATRICK CHAPPATTE, International Herald Tribune

SANDY HUFFAKER
Cagle Cartoons

MIKE LANE, Baltimore Sun

MONTE WOLVERTON, Cagle Cartoons

JEFF PARKER, Florida Today

THESE CORPORATE SCANDALS AND QUESTIONS CONCERNING YOUR PAST BUSINESS RECORD HAVE YOUR STOCK FALLING IN THE LATEST POLLS, MR. PRESIDENT...

SELL! SELL!

DARYL CAGLE
Slate

WHILE "VACATIONING" AT HIS RANCH IN TEXAS, THE PRESIDENT'S WORK DAY LOOKS VERY MUCH LIKE IT DOES IN WASHINGTON.

PAT BAGLEY, Salt Lake Tribune

MIKE LANE, Baltimore Sun

SANDY HUFFAKER, Cagle Cartoons

SANDY HUFFAKER, Cagle Cartoons

MONTE WOLVERTON, Cagle Cartoons

PATRICK CHAPPATTE, International Herald Tribune

SANDY HUFFAKER, Cagle Cartoons

SANDY HUFFAKER, Cagle Cartoons

Enron

Kenneth Lay, the CEO of Enron, was George W. Bush's biggest campaign contributor. "Kenny Boy," as the president nicknamed him, was caught with both hands in the Enron cookie jar in the biggest business scandal of modern U.S. history.

The Enron scandal was heating up around Groundhog Day in 2001, at the same time the president choked on a pretzel while watching a football game. Cartoonists all drew Bush emerging from his hole to predict six more weeks of scandal or choking on the Enron pretzel, but the Enron disgrace quietly disappeared as it was pushed out of the news spotlight by the 9/11 attacks.

BRIAN FAIRRINGTON, Cagle Cartoons

DARYL CAGLE, Slate

JOHN TREVER, Albuquerque Journal

MONTE WOLVERTON, Cagle Cartoons

43

'SOOoo ... THIS IS THE LINCOLN BEDROOM.'

MILT PRIGGEE, National- Syndicated

BRIAN FAIRRINGTON, Cagle Cartoons

MIKE LANE, Baltimore Sun

DARYL CAGLE
Slate

DARYL CAGLE
Slate

Religion in the White House

President Bush is a born-again Christian, and his strongest support comes from the conservative Christian community. When the president first took office, he barred funds for international agencies that provide abortions and started "faith-based initiatives" that allowed religious charities to run government-funded programs that had been limited to nonreligious contractors in the past—all to the delight of his devoted supporters.

DARYL CAGLE
Honolulu Advertiser

DARYL CAGLE HONOLULU ADVERTISER
www.cagle.com

MIKE KEEFE, Denver Post

CAMERON CARDOW
Ottawa Citizen

BRIAN FAIRRINGTON

J.D. Crowe, Mobile Register

JEFF PARKER, Florida Today

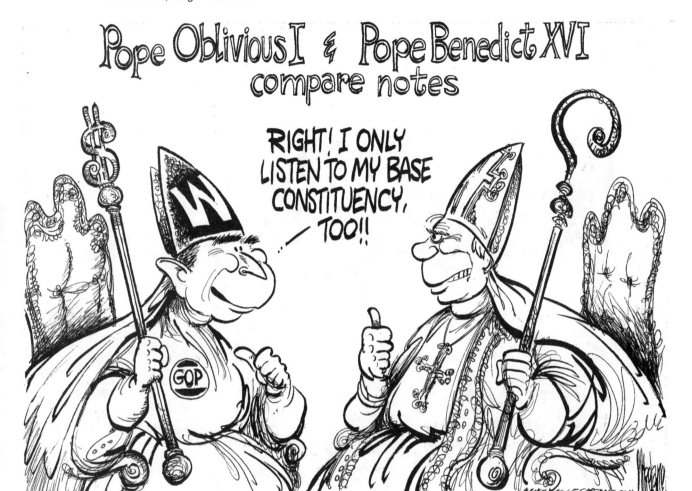

MIKE KEEFE
Denver Post

SANDY HUFFAKER
Cagle Cartoons

RELIGION IN THE WHITE HOUSE

OSMANI SIMANCA
Brazil

MIKE LANE
Baltimore Sun

9/11

R.J. MATSON
New York Observer

© **MATSON** THE NEW YORK OBSERVER

J.D. CROWE
Mobile Register

CHRISTO KOMARNITSKI
Bulgaria

DARYL CAGLE
Slate

56

MIKE KEEFE
Denver Post

PATRICK CHAPPATTE
International Herald Tribune

STAIRWAY to HEAVEN

"The AWAKENING"
SEPTEMBER 11, 2001

J.D. CROWE, Mobile Register

CAMERON CARDOW, Ottawa Citizen

MIKE KEEFE
Denver Post

BRIAN
FAIRRINGTON
Cagle Cartoons

Bush and Osama

The baddest bad guy in the world still hasn't been caught as of the time this book was written. Osama Bin-Ladin was the mastermind behind 9/11 and helped to define the Bush presidency. Osama has gone from being the biggest thorn in the president's side to being ignored as it became clear that he was not going to be caught any time soon. America had Osama in its sights in the hills of Tora Bora, Afghanistan, but he slipped away and faded from public view. Whether dead, sick, or cowering in a cave, no one knows.

OSMANI SIMANCA, Brazil

www.caglecartoons.com/espanol SIMANCA

SANDY HUFFAKER
Cagle Cartoons

OSMANI SIMANCA, Brazil

MIKE LESTER, Rome News-Tribune

DARYL CAGLE
Slate.com

MIKE KEEFE, Denver Post

PETAR PISMESTROVIC, Austria

...FOUR MORE YEARS OF THE SAME!

G. W. BUSH

O. BIN LADEN

ARCADIO ESQUIVEL, Costa Rica

www.caglecartoons.com/espanol

OSMANI SIMANCA, Brazil

"Amazing Similarities"

BETWEEN GEORGE W. BUSH, THE MAN GOD CHOSE TO BE PRESIDENT OF THE UNITED STATES — AND OSAMA BIN LADIN, THE MAN GOD CHOSE TO DEFEAT THE GREAT SATAN

BOTH LIKE TO BLOW THINGS UP

BOTH WON'T TOUCH ALCOHOL EVER SINCE THEY "GOT RELIGION"

BOTH BELIEVE CREATIONISM SHOULD BE TAUGHT IN SCHOOLS

BOTH KNOW GOD IS ON THEIR SIDE

BOTH ARE CONFIDENT, DECISIVE AND NEVER ADMIT MAKING A MISTAKE

BOTH OPPOSE GUN CONTROL

BOTH SPEND THEIR SPARE TIME HANGING AROUND IN THE DESERT.

BOTH WERE BORN INTO POWERFUL FAMILIES

BOTH WANT EACH OTHER DEAD

BOTH ARE RICH

BOTH OPPOSE GAY MARRIAGE

BOTH OPPOSE EMBRYONIC STEM CELL RESEARCH

BOTH DO LOTS OF BUSINESS WITH THEIR FRIENDS IN SAUDI ARABIA

BOTH MISPRONOUNCE THE WORD "NUCLEAR"

SADDAM HUSSEIN DIDN'T LIKE BOTH OF THEM

NEITHER READS THE NEWSPAPER

DARYL CAGLE SLATE.COM   DARYL CAGLE, Slate

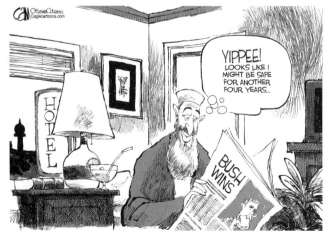

CAMERON CARDOW, Ottawa Citizen

www.caglecartoons.com/espanol

OSMANI SIMANCA, Brazil

CAMERON CARDOW, Ottawa Citizen

NIGHT OF THE LIVING DEAD

RIBER HANSSON, Sweden

PATRICK CHAPPATTE, International Herald Tribune

PETAR PISMESTROVIC, Austria

M.e. COHEN

PETAR PISMESTROVIC, Austria

CAMERON CARDOW, Ottawa Citizen

Bush and Terrorism

President Bush had the misfortune of being in office during a worldwide terrorism Renaissance: the 9/11 attacks, bombs on trains in Madrid, bombs in subways in London, a massacre at a school in Russia, a nightclub bombing in Bali, and daily bombings in Iraq. The world was forced to become accustomed to constant fear and increased levels of security.

ARES, Cuba

MIKE LANE, Cagle Cartoons

PETAR PISMESTROVIC
Austria

PATRICK CHAPPATTE, International Herald Tribune

MIKE KEEFE
Denver Post

OLLE JOHANSSON, Sweden

BUSH AND TERRORISM

LARRY WRIGHT, Detroit News

ANGEL BOLIGAN, Mexico

MONTE WOLVERTON, Cagle Cartoons

The 9/11 Excuse

WE ARE CLEAR-CUTTING NATIONAL FORESTS SO THE TERRORISTS WON'T HAVE A PLACE TO HIDE!

RATS!

www.caglecartoons.com

MIKE LANE
Baltimore Sun

DANCE SCHOOL "WAR AGAINST TERROR"

AFGHANISTAN...

...IRAQ...

...IRAN...

AND SO ON...

PETAR PISMESTROVIC
Austria

JOHN TREVER, Albuquerque Journal

OLLE JOHANSSON, Sweden

PETAR PISMESTROVIC, Austria

Bush and the United Nations

The United Nations was a nettlesome problem for the Bush administration. U.N. officials lined their pockets with Saddam's "Oil for Food" money, while the Iraqi people continued to go hungry. The U.N. made it tough for the U.S. to get into the war with Iraq but ironically also provided a reason for war: Iraq wasn't complying with U.N. sanctions. Conservatives have long despised the U.N., and President Bush threw a bone to his conservative supporters by appointing John Bolton, an outspoken critic of the U.N., to the post of United Nations ambassador, over the loud objections of Democrats.

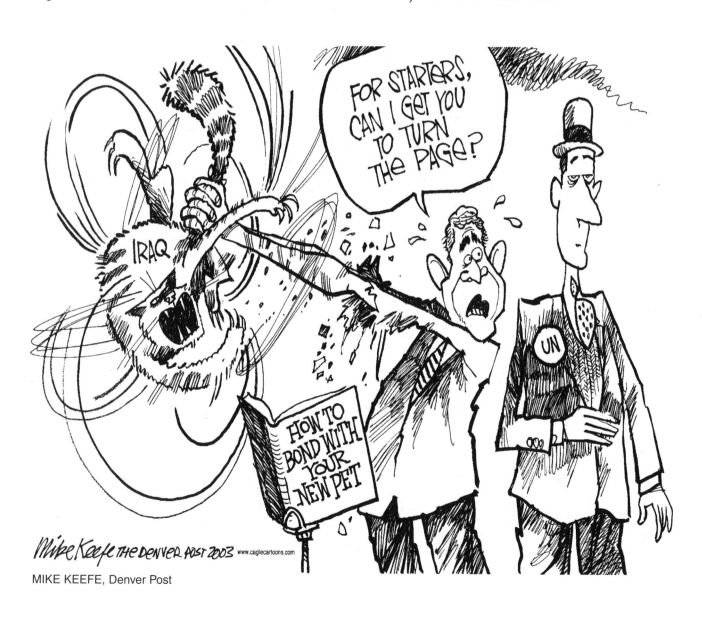

MIKE KEEFE, Denver Post

JOHN TREVER, Albuquerque Journal

DARYL CAGLE
Slate

CAMERON CARDOW, Ottawa Citizen

ARES, Cagle Cartoons

SANDY HUFFAKER

MIKE LANE, Baltimore Sun

LARRY WRIGHT, Detroit News

MIKE LESTER, Rome News-Tribune

ARES

PATRICK CHAPPATTE, International Herald Tribune

MIKE LESTER, Rome News-Tribune

UNWILLING TO SETTLE FOR ANYTHING OTHER
THAN FIRST PLACE STATUS IN THE WORLD
COMMUNITY, PRESIDENT BUSH ANNOUNCES
TO THE U.N. GENERAL ASSEMBLY THAT IT
IS THE AMERICANS AND NOT THE POLES WHO
DESERVE THE REPUTATION OF BEING TOP DRAWER
IMBECILES CELEBRATED IN STORY AND SONG.

DWAYNE BOOTH
Mr. Fish

MIKE LANE, Baltimore Sun

DARYL CAGLE
Slate

78

JOHN TREVER, Albuquerque Journal

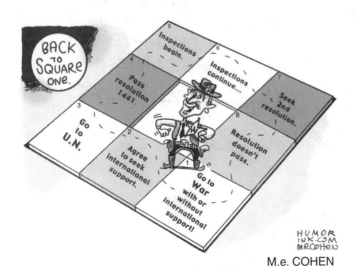

M.e. COHEN

THOMAS BOLDT, Calgary Sun

Icy Europe

President Bush was not popular in Europe, where he was seen as a trigger-happy cowboy-buffoon. The American audience found the president's misuse of words to be a charming dyslexia that made him seem more warmly human, Europeans cringed. Where Americans feel comforted by the president's born-again faith, Europeans recoiled. President Bush didn't get along well with French President Chirac or German Chancellor Schroeder, but he became good buddies with British Prime Minister Blair, Italian Prime Minister Berlusconi, and Spanish Prime Minister Aznar, to the disgust of the British, Italian, and Spanish people.

DARYL CAGLE
Slate

STEPHANE PERAY
Thailand

SANDY HUFFAKER, Cagle Cartoons

81

OLLE JOHANSSON
Sweden

JOHN TREVER
Albuquerque Journal

MIKE LANE
Baltimore Sun

DARYL CAGLE
Slate

MIKE LANE
Baltimore Sun

DARYL CAGLE
Slate

PETAR PISMETROVIC, Austria

R.J. MATSON
New York
Observer

"GRAB A BRUSH, TONY, AND I'LL SHOW YOU HOW WE MEND FENCES IN AMERICA!"

www.caglecartoons.com/espanol SIMANCA

OSMANI SIMANCA
Brazil

PATRICK CHAPPATTE
International Herald Tribune

PETAR PISMESTROVIC
Austria

CHRISTO KOMARNITSKI
Bulgaria

DARYL CAGLE
Slate

OSMANI SIMANCA
Brazil

www.caglecartoons.com/espanol

Bush and Saddam

This is the guy who tried to kill President Bush's dad. Whether he had weapons of mass destruction or not, he had to go. The president's relationship with Saddam had three parts: the buildup to war with sanctions and searches for weapons of mass destruction, the invasion of Iraq with Saddam in hiding, and Saddam's capture. Saddam never seemed to "get it;" at one point he even challenged President Bush to a debate.

DARYL CAGLE, Slate

DARYL CAGLE, Slate

JUST WHAT WE NEED.

DARYL CAGLE, Slate

89

PETAR PISMESTROVIC, Kleine Zeitung, Austria

EMAD HAJJAJ, Jordan

MIKE LANE, Cagle Cartoons

BRIAN FAIRRINGTON, Cagle Cartoons

MILT PRIGGEE, National-Syndicated

EMAD HAJJAJ, Jordan

MIKE KEEFE
Denver Post

MIKE KEEFE
Denver Post

MIKE LANE
Baltimore Sun

SANDY HUFFAKER
Cagle Cartoons

MONTE WOLVERTON, Cagle Cartoons

MIKE LANE, Baltimore Sun

RIBER HANSSON
Sweden

PATRICK CHAPPATTE, International Herald Tribune

CAM CARDOW, Ottawa Citizen

DARYL CAGLE, Slate

94

ALEN LAUZAN, Chile

OSMANI SIMANCA, Brazil

MIKE LESTER, Rome News-Tribune

Mission Accomplished

Photo opportunities make the best backdrops for satire. The Bush administration's biggest "photo-op" came when the president landed a plane on the deck of the USS Abraham Lincoln, dressed in a pilot's flight suit, declaring that major combat operations in Iraq were over. An American flag waved proudly overhead and a large banner hung in the background reading "Mission Accomplished." The crowd of nearly 1000 men cheered.

Since that day more than 1800 American soldiers have died in Iraq.

DARYL CAGLE, Slate.com

MIKE KEEFE
Denver Post

MISSION ACCOMPLISHED!

POST-WAR

MISSION ACCOMPLIS

JEFF PARKER,
Florida Today
caglecartoons.com
©2004 FLORIDA TODAY

MKE LANE
Cagle Cartoons

MIKE KEEFE
Denver Post

VINCE O'FARRELL, Illawarra Mercury, Australia

LARRY WRIGHT, Detroit News

MIKE KEEFE, Denver Post

Abu Ghraib Photos

President Bush was surprised by the Abu Ghraib prison scandal, which ended any hope of winning over the hearts and minds of the Iraqi people. Photos surfaced showing the abuse of Iraqi prisoners by American soldiers and fueled an already heated debate over the ongoing conflict in Iraq. The photos were shown all over the world, where many saw them as recruiting posters for terrorism.

caglecartoons.com/espanol

ANGEL BOLIGAN
Mexico

LARRY WRIGHT
Detroit News

MIKE LANE
Cagle Cartoons

103

ARES.

caglecartoons.com/espanol

PATRICK CHAPPATTE
International Herald Tribune

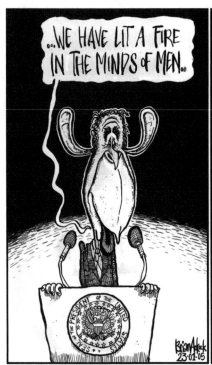

BRIAN ADCOCK
Scotland

EMAD HAJJAJ
Jordan

106

RIBER HANSSON
Sweden

THE CHICKENS COME HOME TO ROOST HERE.

JEFF PARKER
Florida Today

caglecartoons.com

WMDs?

During the buildup to war with Iraq, the president repeatedly warned Americans of the dangers of Saddam Hussein's stockpiles of weapons of mass destruction ("WMDs"). Despite a thorough search, no WMDs were found in Iraq, and the Bush administration very reluctantly came to the conclusion that the WMDs were never really there.

MONTE WOLVERTON, Cagle Cartoons

BOB ENGLEHART
Hartford Courant

DARYL CAGLE, Slate

caglecartoons.com

LARRY WRIGHT
Detroit News

109

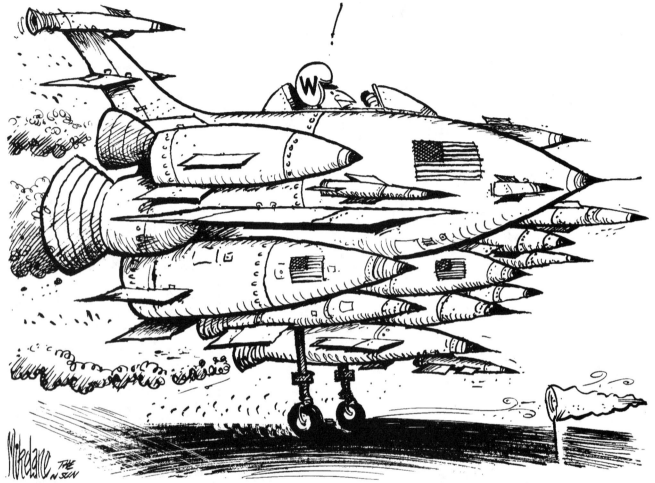

MIKE KEEFE, Denver Post

CAMERON CARDOW, Ottawa Citizen

CAMERON CARDOW, Ottawa Citizen

MIKE KEEFE
Denver Post

CONGRESSMAN, I RESPECTFULLY DECLINE TO ANSWER IRAQ-WMD QUESTIONS...

ON THE CONSTI-TUTIONAL GROUNDS THAT...

MY ANSWERS MIGHT TEND TO...

WWW.CAGLECARTOONS.COM

KEEP ME FROM GETTING RE-ELECTED...

MIKE LANE, Baltimore Sun

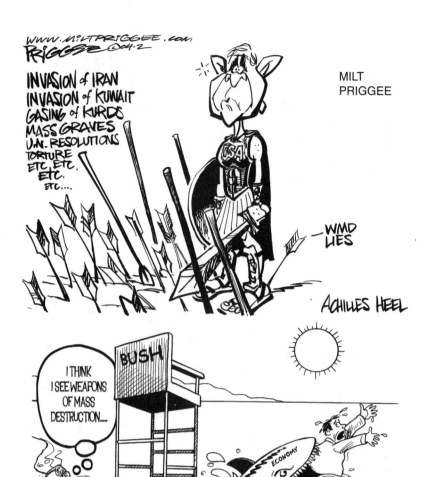

WWW.MILTPRIGGEE.COM
PRIGGEE ©04.2

INVASION of IRAN
INVASION of KUWAIT
GASING of KURDS
MASS GRAVES
U.N. RESOLUTIONS
TORTURE
ETC. ETC.
ETC.
ETC....

MILT PRIGGEE

WMD LIES

ACHILLES HEEL

I THINK I SEE WEAPONS OF MASS DESTRUCTION...

BUSH

ECONOMY

ARCADIO ESQUIVEL, Costa Rica
WWW.CAGLECARTOONS.COM/ESPANOL
2004-02-12

NO WMD

IRAQ

OLLE JOHANSSON
Sweden

CAMERON CARDOW, Ottawa Citizen

MIKE KEEFE
Denver Post

113

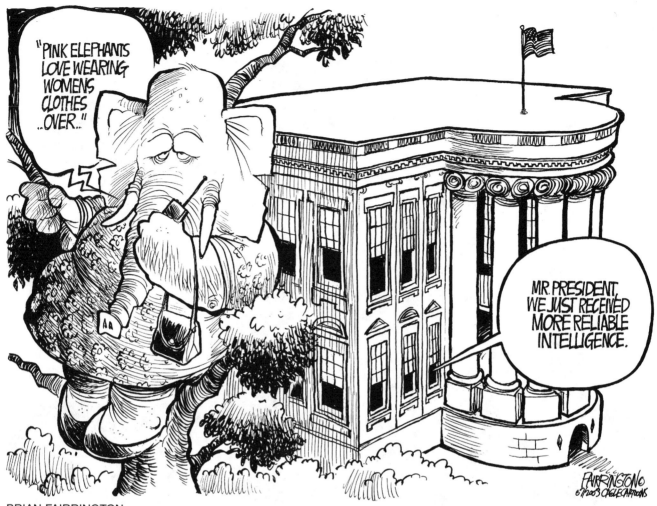

BRIAN FAIRRINGTON
Cagle Cartoons

BOB ENGLEHART
Hartford Courant

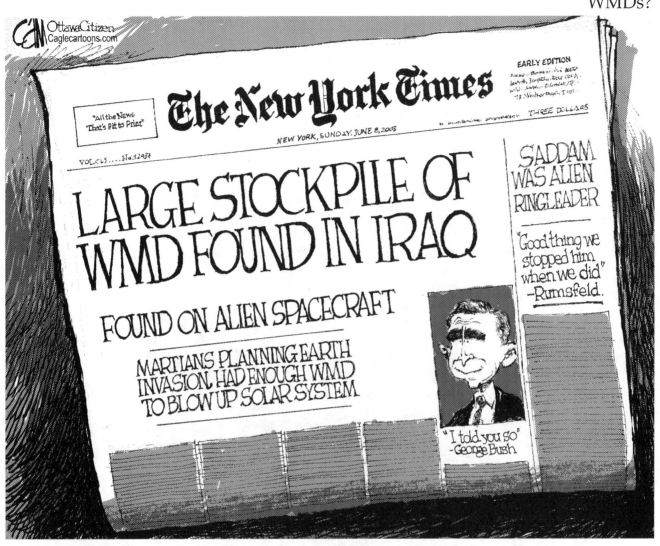

CAMERON CARDOW
Ottawa Citizen

MONTE WOLVERTON
Cagle Cartoons

Tax Cuts

The president's father George H.W. Bush is best remembered for saying the words, "Read my lips: no new taxes!" shortly before he raised taxes. The younger president Bush would not repeat the same mistake.

George W. Bush is not only the biggest spending president in history, but also the biggest tax-cutting president in American history—and the only one to cut taxes in a time of war. Critics argued that the Bush tax cuts went disproportionately to the wealthy, but middle class families were pleased to find some extra dollars in their refunds, too. The tax cuts were also handed out liberally to the president's corporate supporters.

MIKE LANE
Baltimore Sun

MONTE WOLVERTON, Cagle Cartoons

MIKE LANE, Baltimore Sun

www.caglecartoons.com *Mike Keefe THE Denver Post 2003*

MIKE KEEFE, Denver Post

117

"I'VE DOWNSIZED. I'VE OUTSOURCED. I'VE SLASHED BENEFITS. RAIDED PENSION FUNDS. I'VE RAISED PRODUCTIVITY, LOWERED STANDARDS, AND I *STILL* CAN'T PAY MY DEBTS!"

R.J. MATSON, The New York Observer

DARYL CAGLE, Slate

MIKE KEEFE, Denver Post

MIKE LANE, Baltimore Sun

JOHN TREVER, Albuquerque Journal

PAT BAGLEY, Salt Lake Tribune

SANDY HUFFAKER, Cagle Cartoons

MIKE KEEFE, Denver Post

SANDY HUFFAKER
Cagle Cartoons

MONTE WOLVERTON, Cagle Cartoons

MIKE LANE, Cagle Cartoons

MIKE LANE
Baltimore Sun

www.caglecartoons.com

MONTE WOLVERTON, Cagle Cartoons

caglecartoons.com

Bush's Mission to Mars

In a grand initiative on the scale of the effort to put a man on the moon in the 1960s, President Bush announced that America would throw its resources behind a manned mission to Mars—that is, until the president and America forgot about the idea a couple of weeks later.

CAMERON CARDOW, Ottawa Citizen

WEAPONS OF MARS DESTRUCTION

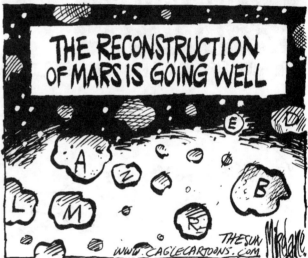

MIKE LANE, Baltimore Sun

MIKE KEEFE, Denver Post

JEFF PARKER
Florida Today

"THE GIANT LEAP?...NO, THIS IS THE SMALL STEP... THE GIANT LEAP COMES WHEN WE ADD UP THE COSTS."

SANDY HUFFAKER, Cagle Cartoons   WWW.CAGLECARTOONS.COM

MIKE LESTER, Rome News-Tribune

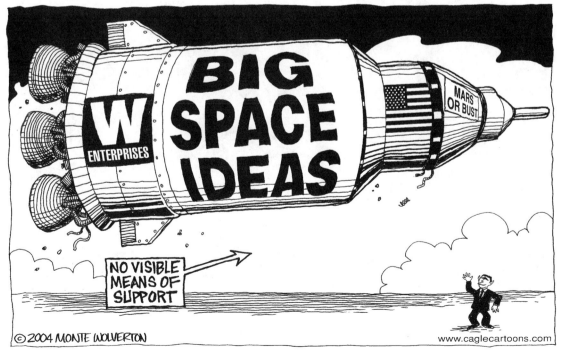

MONTE
WOLVERTON
Cagle Cartoons

Gay Marriage

President Bush is very popular among homophobic voters, and he supported a constitutional amendment banning gay marriage. The President's political "architect" Karl Rove worked to place anti-gay–rights initiatives on the ballots in swing states during the 2004 election. The strategy worked, bringing large numbers of voters opposed to the civil rights of homosexuals, boosting the president in important, tight races.

HOPING TO IMPRESS HIS GOD EVEN MORE THAN HE ALREADY HAS, PRESIDENT BUSH DECIDES TO STRENGTHEN THE PROPOSED AMENDMENT TO THE CONSTITUTION BANNING GAY MARRIAGE BY MODELING ITS RESTRICTIONS ON THE EARLIEST EXAMPLE OF THE CREATION MYTH, NAMELY THE INCEST AS PRACTICED BY THE CHILDREN OF ADAM AND EVE, AND MAKING THE ONLY LEGITIMATE UNION RECOGNIZED IN AMERICA THAT BETWEEN A MAN AND HIS SISTER.

MR. FISH

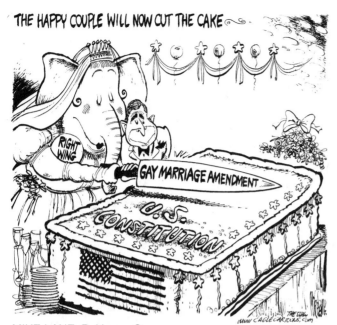

MIKE LANE, Baltimore Sun

MILT PRIGGEE

BRIAN FAIRRINGTON, Cagle Cartoons

LARRY WRIGHT, Detroit News

MIKE KEEFE, Denver Post

BRIAN FAIRRINGTON
Cagle Cartoons

MONTE WOLVERTON
Cagle Cartoons

MIKE KEEFE, Denver Post

SANDY HUFFAKER
Cagle Cartoons

Bush and the Economy

Spending and tax cuts! The economy is simple for President Bush.

"... MEANWHILE, AMERICANS WHO HAVE JOBS CLING TO THEM DESPERATELY ..."

MIKE LANE, Baltimore Sun

JOHN TREVER, Albuquerque Journal

MIKE KEEFE
Denver Post

133

OLLE JOHANSSON, Sweden

MIKE KEEFE, Denver Post

JOHN TREVER, Albuquerque Journal

DARYL CAGLE
Slate

MIKE KEEFE
Denver Post

135

DARYL CAGLE
Slate

MIKE KEEFE, Denver Post

BRIAN FAIRRINGTON
Cagle Cartoons

www.cagelcartoons

MIKE LANE, Cagle Cartoons

PETAR PISMESTROVIC, Austria

DARYL CAGLE, Slate

PETAR PISMESTROVIC
Austria

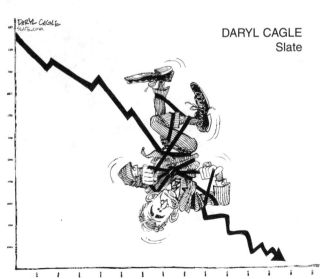

DARYL CAGLE
Slate

LARRY WRIGHT, Detroit News

MIKE LANE, Baltimore Sun

MIKE KEEFE, Denver Post

MONTE WOLVERTON, Cagle Cartoons

Bush and His Cabinet

President Bush's cabinet was filled with cartoon characters. Cartoonists wondered who was truly pulling the strings: W. or his second-in-command, Vice President Dick Cheney. National Security Advisor, and later Secretary of State, Condoleezza Rice put a happy face on the president's policies, along with deadpan Attorney General John Ashcroft, who came into office just after losing an election to a dead man in Missouri. Secretary of Defense Donald Rumsfeld was sometimes less successful with his colorful press conferences. The president demanded complete loyalty from his cabinet. Secretary of State Colin Powell was often rumored to disagree with the administration's hawkish policies—but he didn't come back for the second term. When Treasury Secretary Paul O'Neill disagreed with President Bush, he was booted out the door.

BOB ENGLEHART, Hartford Courant

www.caglecartoons.com/espanol

OSMANI SIMANCA, Brazil

SANDY HUFFAKER, Cagle Cartoons

OF COURSE I FEEL FREE TO DISAGREE WITH THE PRESIDENT.

CONDI BUSH

WWW.CAGLECARTOONS.COM

PETAR PISMESTROVIC, Austria

143

OFFICIAL PORTRAIT OF THE SECRETARY OF STATE'S TRIUMPHANT RETURN TO FRANCE

R.J. MATSON, New York Observer

DWAYNE BOOTH, Mr. Fish

R.J. MATSON, New York Observer

MIKE LANE, Baltimore Sun

MONTE WOLVERTON, Cagle Cartoons

CAMERON CARDOW
Ottawa Citizen

RIBER HANSSON, Sweden

JEFF PARKER
Florida Today

U.N. INSPECTORS
FIND EMPTY
WARHEADS
IN IRAQ..

THEY CAN FIND PLENTY MORE OF THEM IN WASHINGTON THESE DAYS...

MIKE KEEFE
Denver Post

The Bush Cabinet: Looking Like a history of America ...

R.J. MATSO, New York Observer

MIKE KEEFE, Denver Post

MIKE KEEFE, Denver Post

MIKE KEEFE, Denver Post

MIKE LANE, Baltimore Sun

VINCE O'FARRELL
Australia

www.caglecartoons.com

MIKE KEEFE, Denver Post

MIKE KEEFE, Denver Post

MIKE LANE, Baltimore Sun

MIKE KEEFE, Denver Post

MIKE KEEFE, Denver Post

ANDY SINGER
No Exit

Social Security

President Bush pushed hard to reform the Social Security system, but his ideas couldn't find any traction. The president wanted to set up private accounts so that workers could invest their Social Security funds in the private sector. Of course, the government spends all the money that comes into the Social Security system, and returns only IOUs to workers' accounts. Democrats objected to the idea that Social Security beneficiaries might risk their retirement funds on an unpredictable stock market and complained that the Medicare system was in more need of repair than Social Security. In the end, no one could agree on a plan, and nothing changed.

SANDY HUFFAKER

"HELLO, POLICE? I'M SUPPOSED TO BE MARRIED TO THE PRESIDENT'S SOCIAL SECURITY PLAN... BUT I'VE BEEN KIDNAPPED!"

MIKE LANE, Cagle Cartoons

HOW DO YOU KNOW YOU DON'T LIKE A BIKINI UNLESS YOU TRY IT ON?

JOHN COLE
Scranton Times

MIKE KEEFE, Denver Post

JEFF PARKER, Florida Today

THE GEORGE W. BUSH SOCIAL SECURITY ☆☆☆ DOG AND PONY SHOW ☆☆☆ FOR AMERICA!!!

THE DOG DIED AND THE PONY'S NOT FEELING AT ALL WELL......

MIKE LANE
Cagle Cartoons

SANDY HUFFAKER
Cagle Cartoons

"IF HE SAYS WE'LL BE WELCOMED WITH CANDY AND FLOWERS, I'M OUTTA HERE!"

R.J. MATSON, Roll Call

MIKE KEEFE
Denver Post

BOB ENGLEHART, Hartford Courant

MONTE WOLVERTON, Cagle Cartoons

MIKE LANE, Cagle Cartoons

MIKE LESTER, Rome News-Tribune (GA)

LARRY WRIGHT, Detroit News

BOB ENGLEHART
Hartford Courant

JOHN TREVER, Albuquerque Journal

LARRY WRIGHT, Detroit News

"One of America's most important institutions- a symbol of the trust between generations- is also in need of wise and effective reform."-From the President's State of the Union speech.

M.e. Cohen@Humorink.com 02.03.05

M.e. COHEN

IDENTITY THEFT!

BACK OFF, BUSH!!

DON'T MESS WITH SOCIAL SECURITY!

DON'T MESS WITH SOCIAL SECURITY!

BACK OFF, BUSH!

MIKE LANE, Cagle Cartoons

I HAVE GOOD NEWS AND BAD NEWS.

GIVE ME THE BAD NEWS FIRST.

BLACKS DON'T LIVE AS LONG AS WHITES.

WHAT'S THE GOOD NEWS?

YOU'LL MAKE MONEY ON PRIVATIZED SOCIAL SECURITY!

OH...

I THOUGHT YOU WERE GOING TO SAY THIS IS YOUR LAST TERM!

BOB ENGLEHART, Hartford Courant

SOCIAL SECURITY

PRIVATIZATION

caglecartoons.com   ©2004 MONTE WOLVERTON

MONTE WOLVERTON, Cagle Cartoons

HAUTE INVESTMENTS INC.

YOU'LL HAVE TO EXCUSE MR. BUYENSELL. HE'S ONE OF OUR BROKERS AND ALWAYS SALIVATES LIKE THAT WHENEVER ANYONE MENTIONS BUSH'S SOCIAL SECURITY PRIVATIZATION PLAN...

caglecartoons.com

JEFF PARKER, Florida Today

"WE SHALL MAKE THE MOST LASTING PROGRESS IF WE RECOGNIZE THAT SOCIAL SECURITY CAN FURNISH ONLY A BASE UPON WHICH EACH ONE OF OUR CITIZENS MAY BUILD HIS INDIVIDUAL SECURITY THROUGH HIS OWN INDIVIDUAL EFFORTS..."

WHO SAID THAT? "W"?

NOPE. "FDR".

NEWS - BUSH URGES CONGRESS TO BACK SOCIAL SECURITY CHANGE

MIKE LESTER, Rome News-Tribune

161

MIKE LANE, Cagle Cartoons

LARRY WRIGHT
Detroit News

MONTE WOLVERTON, Cagle Cartoons

LARRY WRIGHT, Detroit News

M.e. COHEN

JOHN TREVER, Albuquerque Journal

OLLE JOHANSSON, Sweden

R.J. MATSON, Roll Call

"MAYBE IT'S TIME TO RECONSIDER OUR BARNSTORMING APPROACH."

R.J. MATSON
Roll Call

MIKE KEEFE, Denver Post
www.caglecartoons.com

Mike Keefe THE DENVER POST 2004

JUST LIKE LAST TERM:
• INVENT A CRISIS.
• EXPLOIT THE PANIC.
• PLAY ON FEARS.

WE HAVE EVIDENCE OF DIRECT LINKS BETWEEN al-Qaeda AND THE SOCIAL SECURITY SYSTEM!

M.e. COHEN

J.D. CROWE
Mobile Register

JOHN COLE

MIKE LANE
Cagle Cartoons

LARRY WRIGHT
Detroit News

LARRY WRIGHT
Detroit News

"...AND THIS TIME IT VANISHED QUITE SLOWLY, BEGINNING WITH THE END OF THE TAIL, AND
ENDING WITH THE GRIN, WHICH REMAINED FOR SOME TIME AFTER THE REST OF IT HAD GONE"

MIKE LANE
Cagle Cartoons

Bush and Putin

After first meeting Russian President Vladimir Putin, President Bush said those famous words, "I looked the man in the eye. I found him to be very straightforward and trustworthy. We had a very good dialogue. I was able to get a sense of his soul." President Bush trusted his personal feelings about people and thought of the Russian president as a good friend. Putin, a former head of the Russian KGB, went on to scale back press freedoms in Russia, bringing back a more centralized, authoritarian regime that had little tolerance for dissent.

CAMERON CARDOW
Ottawa Citizen

OttawaCitizen
Caglecartoons.com

J.D. CROWE, Mobile Register

BOB ENGLEHART, Hartford Courant

MIKE KEEFE, Denver Post

JOHN TREVER, Albuquerque Journal

CHRISTO KOMARNITSKI, Bulgaria

169

CHRISTO KOMARNITSKI, Sofia, Bulgaria

MIKE KEEFE, Denver Post

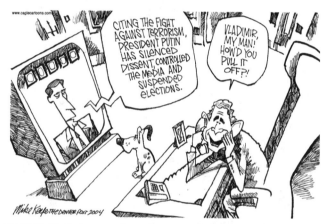

MIKE KEEFE, Denver Post

M.e. COHEN

OLLE JOHANSSON, Sweden

MONTE WOLVERTON, Cagle Cartoons

SANDY HUFFAKER, National

JOHN COLE

171

Stem Cell Research

Former First Lady Nancy Reagan urged the president to support embryonic stem cell research, highlighting the divide on the issue, even within the Republican party. For President Bush, a fertilized egg has a soul and to use the egg in research would be murder. Critics of embryonic stem cell research come from the pro-life community and are among the president's core supporters. They claim that the science has no value and that stem cell research can be done without "killing babies." From the point of view of most Americans (and most scientists) embryonic stem cell research is an important area for research, holding the promise of cures for many terrible diseases.

OSMANI SIMANCA, Brazil

STEMCELL HARDHEAD

www.caglecartoons.com/espanol

172

DARYL CAGLE
Slate

DARYL CAGLE
Slate

MIKE KEEFE, Denver Post

MIKE KEEFE, Denver Post

MIKE LANE
Cagle Cartoons

LARRY WRIGHT, Detroit News

M.e. COHEN

LARRY WRIGHT, Detroit News

Campaign 2004

At first glance, the 2004 presidential election seemed strangely familiar: George W. Bush faced another wooden Democrat and won by another slim margin. But this time around, the presidential election was tame; there were no lawsuits, no fiery speeches on the Senate floor, no final Supreme Court decision, and President Bush actually won a majority of the votes.

CAMERON CARDOW, Ottawa Citizen

DARYL CAGLE, Slate

THOMAS BOLDT, Calgary Sun

THOMAS BOLDT, Calgary Sun

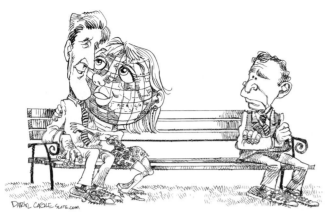

DARYL CAGLE, Slate

GEORGE W. BUSH HAVING HIS HEAD EXAMINED TO SEE IF HE IS COMPETENT ENOUGH TO SERVE A SECOND TERM.

PROCTOLOGY

DWAYNE BOOTH
Mr. Fish

MR. FISH

JOHN COLE
Durham Herald-Sun

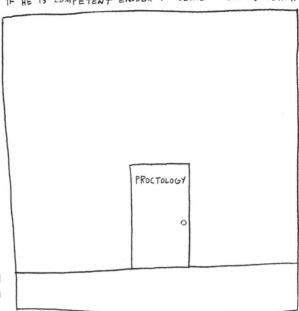

WASN'T KERRY THE ONE WITH THE WEIRD FACIAL COLOR?

IRAQ WAS JUST A DIVERSION FROM THE WAR ON TERROR

DEBATE #1

MIKE LANE, Cagle Cartoons

CAMERON CARDOW, Ottawa Citizen

MIKE KEEFE, Denver Post

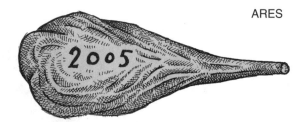

ARES

ARES.

4 MORE YEARS

SANDY HUFFAKER, Cagle Cartoons

MIKE KEEFE, Denver Post

VINCE O'FARRELL, Australia

PATRICK CHAPPATTE, International Herald Tribune

BRIAN ADCOCK, Scotland

DARYL CAGLE, Slate

MIKE LANE, Baltimore Sun

VINCE O'FARRELL, Australia

MIKE KEEFE, Denver Post

OLLE JOHANSSON, Sweden

LARRY WRIGHT, Detroit News

MIKE LANE, Cagle Cartoons

RIBER HANSSON
Sweden

YOUR POLLS ARE SLIPPING IN ALL AREAS EXCEPT THE SUPREME COURT WHICH REMAINS A ROCK SOLID 5-4...

ALL RIGHT!!

'04

WWW.CAGLECARTOONS.COM

MIKE LANE, Cagle Cartoons

FOUR MORE YEARS...

www.caglecartoons.com

VINCE O'FARRELL, Australia

183

THE BUSH CAMPAIGN REACHES OUT TO THE FEMALE VOTER...

MIKE LESTER, Rome News-Tribune

M.e. COHEN

JOHN TREVER, Albuquerque Journal

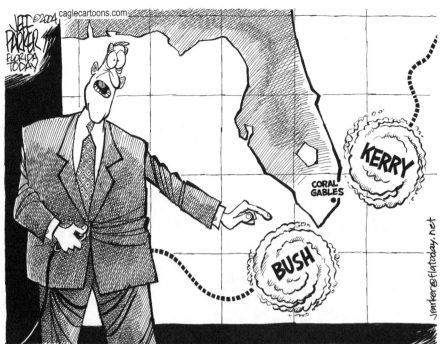

"...AND THE TWO ARE EXPECTED TO CONVERGE ON CORAL GABLES SOMETIME THURSDAY EVENING, SO WE'RE EXPECTING TO SEE LOTS OF **WIND AND MUD**..."

JEFF PARKER
Florida Today

MIKE LANE, Cagle Cartoons

185

MIKE LANE, Baltimore Sun

VINCE O'FARRELL, Australia

MILT PRIGGEE

R.J. MATSON, New York Observer

"ROUND ONE, LADIES AND GENTLEMEN, THE JUMPSUIT COMPETITION!"

R.J. MATSON, New York Observer

CAMERON CARDOW, Ottawa Citizen

"I DON'T KNOW WHETHER TO GIVE YOU GUYS AN "A" OR AN "F"!"

R.J. MATSON
New York Observer

SANDY HUFFAKER
Cagle Cartoons

MIKE LESTER
Rome News-Tribune

DARYL CAGLE
Slate

SANDY HUFFAKER, Cagle Cartoons

LARRY WRIGHT, Detroit News

MONTE WOLVERTON, Cagle Cartoons

R.J. MATSON
Roll Call

"TOO BAD YOU CAN'T VOTE AGAINST THE GUY AFTER YOU'VE VOTED FOR HIM."

CAMERON CARDOW
Ottawa Citizen

LARRY WRIGHT, Detroit News

THOMAS BOLDT, Calgary Sun

THOMAS BOLDT, Calgary Sun

WASN'T KERRY THE ONE WITH THE WEIRD FACIAL COLOR?

DEBATE #1

THE END IS NEAR!

the 2nd term is HERE!

Maybe we can work as a team.

MR. FISH

DWAYNE BOOTH, Mr. Fish

JEFF PARKER, Florida Today

MIKE LANE, Cagle Cartoons

FIRST TERM....

SECOND TERM....

MANDATE

BRIAN ADCOCK, The Scotland, The Prague Post

ACCOUNTABILITY, ACCOUNTABILITY AND ACCOUNTABILITY
— AUDITORS

NOT INVITED TO THE GRAND INAUGURAL...

WWW.CAGLECARTOONS.COM

I win!

DEFICITS

TERRORISM

IRAN

PROLIFERATION

IRAQ

WAR

EUROPE

MIKE LANE
Cagle Cartoons

WWW.CAGLECARTOONS.COM

MEANWHILE..AT THE INAUGURATION OF GEORGE W. BUSH...

NOW RAISE YOUR RIGHT HAND AND REPEAT AFTER ME...

AFTER ME.. AFTER ME .. AFTER ME.. AFTER ME.. AFTER ME...

FOR THE NEXT FOUR YEARS WE WILL SPREAD LIBERTY AND FREEDOM TO THE DARKEST CORNERS OF THE WORLD..

LOAD FREEDOM!

CAMERON CARDOW, Ottawa Citizen

$73 TRILLION DEBT $

FLOATS YOU PROBABLY WON'T SEE IN THE INAUGURATION PARADE...

JEFF PARKER, Florida Today

Showdown with Sheehan

Cindy Sheehan, the grieving mother of a soldier who was killed in Iraq, ignited a lively protest against the Iraq war by camping out at the president's ranch in Crawford, Texas. She demanded to speak to the president and insisted that she would stay at the camp until the president agreed to meet with her.

Sheehan's camp soon turned into a media circus as she became the focus of the opposition to the war. The president's defenders painted Sheehan as a radical leftist, pointing out that she had met with the president once before and drawing attention to her more outrageous statements.

THOMAS BOLDT
Calgary Sun

MIKE KEEFE, Denver Post

MIKE LESTER
Rome News-Tribune

CINDY SHEEHAN'S LIST of DEMANDS:

- TROOPS OUT OF IRAQ
- IMPEACH BUSH
- BUSH TO JAIL
- ISRAEL OUT OF PALESTINE
- I'M NOT PAYING TAXES

"WHY IS THAT DEAD SOLDIER'S MOM PICKING ON ME?"

R.J. MATSON
St. Louis Post Dispatch

DARYL CAGLE
MSNBC.com

SHOWDOWN WITH SHEEHAN

CAMERON CARDOW
Ottawa Citizen

MIKE LESTER
Rome News-Tribune

VINCE O'FARRELL
Australia

DARYL CAGLE
MSNBC.com

Hurricane Katrina

The biggest natural disaster in history flattened the Gulf Coast and caused a flood that virtually destroyed the city of New Orleans. America watched horrific scenes on television for days before aid reached the hurricane victims.

DARYL CAGLE
MSNBC.com

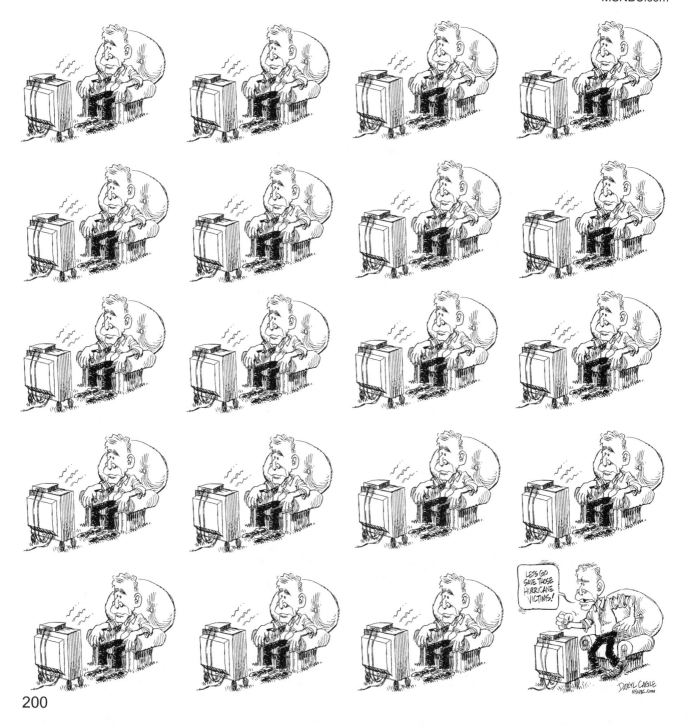

PATRICK CHAPPATTE
International Herald
Tribune

BOB ENGLEHART
Hartford Courant

PATRICK CHAPPATTE, International Herald Tribune

STEPHANE PERAY, Thailand

CHRISTO KOMARNITSKI
Bulgaria

MARIE WOOLF, Cagle Cartoons

PETER LEWIS
Australia

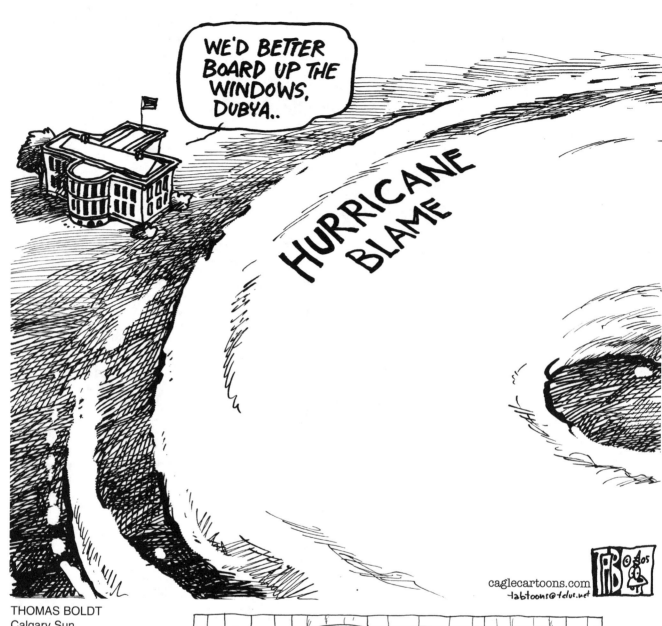

THOMAS BOLDT
Calgary Sun

LARRY WRIGHT
Detroit News

MIKE LANE, Cagle Cartoons

MIKE KEEFE, Denver Post

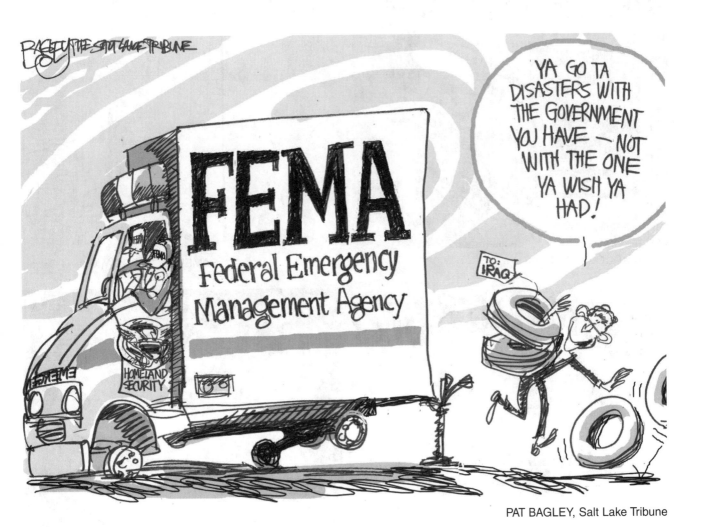

PAT BAGLEY, Salt Lake Tribune

BRIAN ADCOCK, Scotland

CAMERON CARDOW, Ottawa Citizen

R.J. MATSON, St. Louis Post Dispatch

MIKE KEEFE, Denver Post

MIKE LESTER, Rome News-Tribune

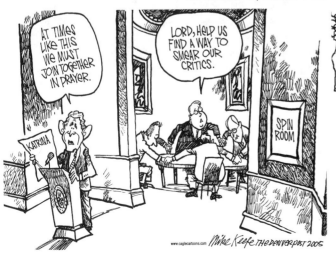

Artists Index

A–B

C

D–E

F-G-H

I-J-K

L

M-N-O

P-Q-R

S-T-U-V

W-X-Y-Z